I Was There...

1066

While this ... based on real characters and actual events,
some ... incidents and people are fictional, created by the author.

Scholastic Children's Books
Euston House,
24 Eversholt Street
London, NW1 1DB, UK

A division of Scholastic Ltd
London ~ New York ~ Toronto ~ Sydney ~ Auckland
Mexico City ~ New Delhi ~ Hong Kong

First published in the UK by Scholastic Ltd, 2015

ISBN 978 1407 14882 3

Printed and bound by CPI Group (UK) Ltd, Croydon, CR0 4YY

1 3 5 7 9 10 8 6 4 2

I Was There...

1066

Jim Eldridge

CHAPTER ONE

CLANG! CLANG! CLANG!

The sounds of sword blades crashing against sword blades, and axes smashing on wooden shields echoed from the battlefield a thousand times over.

I stood on a high ridge with the other young squires, watching. My name is Edwin. I am twelve years old and a squire to my father, Lord Wolf, who is one of the bravest fighters in the court of King Harold, King of England. My job is to keep his spare sword and shield ready should the ones he uses in battle break. I am also there to bring him refreshment when there is a break in the battle, but so far there has been none. Our army, the English army, have been engaged in heavy fighting against the Norwegian King, Harald Hardrada, and his army of Vikings, helped by our own King Harold's treacherous brother, Tostig, for hours. Already the battlefield is strewn with dead from both sides, but more of theirs than ours.

I feel a sense of great pride watching my father in action; his skill as a warrior is clearly on display as he battles the Viking invaders.

We are at a place in the north of England called Stamford Bridge. We marched the hundreds of miles north to this place from Kent in the south as soon as we heard the news that the Norwegians had invaded and were attacking villages and towns, and were heading for the city of York. It is said the Norwegian army was 10,000 men strong. Although the Vikings are known to be fierce warriors, our side had 15,000 soldiers, a huge army, with each man pledging his life to King Harold and the English cause to drive out the invaders.

The battle raged on – swords, spears and heavy axes being wielded by both sides. Then, suddenly, the Vikings began to retreat. They must have known that their attack was lost and only death awaited them. One of their commanders must have decided that it was better for some of their army to survive and escape, rather than lose every man, because slowly but surely the Norwegians were retreating, heading for the river.

"The Viking king has been killed," murmured a voice beside me. It was my best friend, Osric, another of the squires. "And so is Tostig, the traitor. They are both dead."

Without their king, their leader, the Norwegians had no cause left to fight for.

As those of us on the ridge watched, the retreat by the Vikings, at first slow, gathered pace, and finally the Norwegians turned and ran. Our soldiers chased after them, attacking them as they fled.

The battle was won.

CHAPTER TWO

After the battle we buried our own dead, but left the dead Vikings to the crows. That evening, we sat by the fires and listened to the soldiers telling tales of the battle. My father told me that the Vikings who lived had been allowed to take their boats and return to Norway, but only after the two sons of King Harald Hardrada, Olaf and Paul, who had survived the battle, had sworn an oath to King Harold not to attack England again.

"But the danger is not yet over, Edwin," my father said, his tone serious. "There will be a much bigger battle to come against the Normans and Duke William."

I often feel these are confusing times. As long as I can remember, we seem to have been in a state of war with someone, with allegiances switching from one to another, and then back again. My friend, Osric, understands these things – the politics – better than I do.

Osric and I have been friends ever since we were five years old. Our fathers' estates in Kent are next to one another: our house, Wolf Court, is at Sevenoaks, and Osric, whose father is Lord Bane, lives at Bane Hall at Otford, just two miles away.

When we were very small we had tutors come to teach us at our homes, but as soon as we turned five, we were sent to be taught by the monks at a monastery in Sevenoaks. For me it was just a short ride away. Osric was brought by cart at first, driven by a house servant, but he insisted on being able to ride his own horse, and soon he would arrive each morning at the monastery on horseback just like me. We each had a servant to ride with us as protection, because as the sons of lords there was always the danger that we might be taken prisoner and held for ransom.

Our day was split in two: in the morning we had our lessons with the monks, and then in the afternoon we returned to our homes for sword and shield training, as well as archery. We were being taught to read and write, but we were also being trained to be fighters, like our fathers.

As trainee warriors, we first learnt our duties by being pages to our fathers, looking after their weapons, and at the same time we learnt to use weapons of our own.

I must say that the business of learning to be a warrior was the more interesting of our studies for me. It was the exact opposite for Osric. He loved learning. He could read English and French and Latin, and he gobbled up the languages with glee. I could read English and a bit of French, but I struggled with Latin, which was a mystery to me.

Likewise, while Osric's writing was praised for its neatness by the monks, they used to beat me with a leather strap for my poor penmanship because I left splodges of black ink from the nib of my feathered quill on the paper. They made me write out the same words over and over until I had written it in a neat enough way to please them.

At first I used to resent the beatings with the leather strap, but as time passed I learned to bear them, deciding they would make me a stronger warrior.

My school days seem a long time ago now as we stand here looking at the battlefield. It was during our long journey north from Kent to face Harald Hardrada and Tostig that Osric had explained to me why the Viking king was invading England, and why there was the threat from Duke William of Normandy.

"It is all because Edward the Confessor had no children, so there was no heir to the English throne," said Osric.

Edward the Confessor had been King of England until he died earlier this year, in January. Some said he had been a wise and good king, some said he had done little as a king except to build a huge cathedral at Westminster Abbey to show how much he loved God. Osric's father, Lord Bane, had little time for Edward. He preferred warrior kings, like our present King Harold. Lord Bane blamed Edward the Confessor for the present situation we were in, with others trying to claim the throne.

"The man was a coward!" I heard him rage once to my father. "He tried to keep peace by promising everyone they would have the throne when he died!"

"Hush, Bane," cautioned my father. "He

was our king. It does not do to speak ill of royalty."

"I speak as I see it!" shouted Lord Bane.

"He kept the peace during his reign," countered my father.

"And now we have war on two fronts!" argued Lord Bane.

"Many people, including my father, think that Edward the Confessor gave too much to the Normans," explained Osric. "He was very friendly with Duke William. He appointed a Norman as archbishop, and many of the monks and priests in our churches were from Normandy."

"Like some of the monks at our school," I nodded.

"Right," said Osric. "And if you remember, about 15 years ago, Edward the Confessor and King Harold's father, Earl Godwin, were at war with one another."

"I don't remember," I told him, smiling. "I wasn't born at the time. And neither were you."

"Yes, but I remember what people tell me about our history," said Osric. "It's important if we're to understand why things are the way they are."

I shook my head. "It's too much detail for me," I said. "I like to know about how to use a sword and a shield."

"But if you don't understand what happened before, how will you know who to support in a war?" asked Osric.

"I support the King," I said. "It's very simple."

"But which king?" asked Osric. "At the moment there are three making claims to the throne of England. Duke William of Normandy claims that Edward the Confessor promised him the crown of England before he died. The Duke also says that our King Harold swore a solemn oath to him when he was in Normandy, agreeing that William would become King of England."

"Duke William lies," I said.

"Then there's King Harald of Norway," continued Osric. "He says that a long time ago, King Magnus of Norway had made an agreement with the King of England, Harthacanute, that if an English or Norwegian king died without an heir, then the other would become king of both England and Norway."

"King Harold Godwinson is our rightful king," I said firmly. "He was elected by the Witenagemot." The Witenagemot was the council of earls and lords of England.

"That may be," said Osric. "But the others claim King Edward promised them the throne."

"And who do you support?" I demanded. "Are you saying we should give up the throne to a foreign invader just because they say so?"

"No," said Osric. "I believe in King Harold. That's why I'm marching with his army all the way to face the Viking invader."

This was the second time that there had been an attack by the Viking King Harald since King Edward died. The first attack had been led by our King Harold's brother, Tostig, who supported the Norwegian king. Tostig attacked the south-east of England with a fleet of ships, but was forced back. Next his ships and soldiers launched an attack on East Anglia, but again they were defeated. According to my father, Tostig then fled north to Scotland to try and raise another army.

At that point we were most worried about the threat from Normandy. King Harold and his army, including my father and me and Osric and Lord Bane, had gathered on the south coast of England, looking across the Channel to Normandy, waiting and watching for the Norman fleet of Duke William to appear as was threatened.

Our army was large, armed with swords, spears and axes. It was rumoured that Duke William had an army just as large, but his attack was held up because he did not have enough ships to carry them all, and so he had to build a whole fleet. And so we waited. July turned to August, and August turned into September, but still there was no sign of the Normans.

September was also harvest time, and many of King Harold's army were farmers and farm labourers who were bound by law to give service to their king at time of war. But the harvest needed to be gathered in if people were to survive the winter, and so Harold allowed many of his men to return to their farms.

And then, halfway through September, news came that the Norwegian king, Harald Hardrada, and Tostig had invaded northern England with a huge army and had already laid waste to some of the northern towns. The army was now advancing on York.

Immediately, we set off northwards with

King Harold, gathering more men as we travelled, and by the 25th of September, when we met the armies of Harald and Tostig at Stamford Bridge in Yorkshire, our army was 15,000 strong.

The battle was brutal. It was said that the Norwegians had needed 300 ships to bring their invading army to England. Such was the death toll inflicted on the Viking army that only 24 of those ships were needed to take the survivors back to Norway.

As Osric and I sat around the fire in the camp at Stamford Bridge discussing the battle with the other squires, we heard the rush of horse's hooves approaching. We saw a rider pull his horse to a halt near to us, and almost collapse out of his saddle. He and the horse looked exhausted. We ran to him, and he panted hoarsely at us: "Tell the King! Duke William's fleet have landed at Hastings!"

CHAPTER THREE

As my father's squire, I was allowed to be with him when he, the King and the other lords met to discuss battle tactics.

"I fear we have lost the element of surprise with the Normans," my father said, when the Council of War met in the King's tent.

"Perhaps not," replied the King, thoughtfully. "Duke William knows we are here fighting the Norwegians. He will know we have just beaten Harald and Tostig, and he will expect us to spend time here to recover. If we set off now, and make fast time, we can catch him before his defences are ready."

"The men are absolutely exhausted after the battle, sire," cautioned another adviser, Lord Brag. "It is some 300 miles to Hastings. After such a long march, especially one at a fast pace, I have my doubts if they will be fit for battle against Duke William and his Normans, who will all be fresh."

King Harold thought this over, and nodded.

"There is wisdom in your opinions," he said. "But we cannot afford to give William time to make inroads into England. We must prevent him from reaching London."

"Our messengers say that he has encountered resistance from some of our local forces in Kent and Sussex, and has decided to make camp there rather than advance towards London. The word is that he has begun building large castles."

Again, King Harold nodded.

"It is the Norman way," he said. "When they invade a new area, they build castles of wood and earth to ensure they are protected against attacks, before they launch their own attacks. Buildings these castles takes time, and we will take advantage of it. We will head south with our fittest soldiers. The others will follow later, when they are recovered and able to travel.

When we reach London we will gather more men and rebuild our army, while we wait for those who follow us afterwards. A week in London should be enough to gather our full strength. And then we will head for Hastings and drive this invader back into the sea, just as we drove out Harald and Tostig's armies."

The next day our reduced army set off south with King Harold riding at the front.

Behind the King came the housecarls, the King's own personal warriors. Among them was my father, and, as his squire, I had the honour of riding alongside him.

Behind us came the men, marching, swords in scabbards ready by their sides and carrying shields in case of attack. My father said we should cover about 25 miles a day, so it would take us about ten days to reach London. To aid the speed of the march, much of the heavy weaponry our soldiers needed, as well as the heavy chain-mail armour that some of us wore, had been loaded onto carts, which trundled along behind each section.

As we rode together on the first day, my father said: "Edwin, very shortly you will reach your thirteenth birthday."

"Yes," I said. My birthday was just three weeks away.

"I took part in my first battle when I was ten," said my father. "But then, in those days, children as young as six were thought of as soldiers." He turned in his saddle and gave me a serious look as he said: "You have been a good page and a good squire, Edwin. You have learnt all the skills well. You can handle a sword and a spear. You use a shield as well as many a bigger man."

As I heard these words I felt a stirring of excitement. Was my father building to what I hoped he was going to say?

"When we reach Hastings and confront the Norman Duke and his army, there is a decision I must make. Do I send you to join the other squires with the servants, as has been the case before, as at Stamford Bridge these last few days, or do I risk letting you join our ranks in battle?"

"It will be no risk, Father," I promised. "I will not let you down."

"Being in battle is not the same as practising your skills," said my father. "The swords are sharp. The spears will kill. Your enemy will not be stopping his sword from hitting you at the last moment."

"I know, Father," I said. "I have been close enough to battle to know what it means."

"You may die."

"Then I will die protecting my King and country," I said.

"You must use your head," said my father. "You must always consider your opponent, your enemy. Watch their move. An attack with just blind passion will result in your death."

"I know, Father," I said. "You have instructed me always in the importance of thinking under pressure."

"That will help keep you alive," nodded my father. "Just as well as your skill with a sword or a shield."

And so it was agreed that I would become a warrior, fully fledged in the forthcoming battle.

For the rest of the journey I could hardly contain my excitement, but I was nervous as well. I had seen men die in battle and it was not a good sight, but my father and those who had helped train me had all told me that being frightened was part of being a warrior. It helped sharpen your senses, made you more aware of what was happening around you when the battle was at its most intense.

I was about to go into battle.

CHAPTER FOUR

I was so excited about my father's announcement that as soon as we made camp for the night I rushed off to find Osric. I found him by the fire where the cook was preparing food for us all.

"Osric!" I whispered, but my whisper was too loud and it made others turn to look at me. I grabbed Osric by the arm and dragged him away to a place we could talk safely, without being overheard.

"Osric! I have the most terrific news! I am to go into battle when we reach Duke William's army!"

Osric looked at me, his face unhappy, his

eyes troubled.

"Me, too," he said.

"That is wonderful!" I burst out in delight. "We will go into battle together!"

Osric shook his head, his eyes downcast.

"I don't want to go into battle," he said miserably.

I stared at him, stunned.

"But… this is what we've been working towards. All our training as pages and squires!"

"I never wanted to be a warrior," said Osric. "I want to be a monk. To learn about the world. To read and write. To study!"

"But…" I kept staring at him, completely taken aback at this news. "But you were good at the training. With the sword and the spear."

"Only because there was never any real danger," said Osric. "But my heart wasn't in it." He shook his head. "I'm not like you, Edwin. I don't want to fight. I don't want to kill anyone, or be killed or badly wounded."

I let this sink in, and my heart went out to my friend, standing there looking so desperately miserable and unhappy.

"Have you told your father this?" I asked.

Osric nodded.

"He flew into a rage. Told me I was a coward. Said he'd killed his first man when he was just eight years old." He gave a sad laugh. "He thought I'd be happy when he told me I was going into battle!"

"Did you tell him why you don't want to fight? About becoming a monk?"

"Yes, and he said that was a role for the second son, my brother Aidan. The first son, the oldest, has to be the warrior." He shook his head miserably. "I will die on the battlefield."

"No you won't," I promised him. "I will protect you."

Osric looked at me with sad eyes.

"No you won't," he said. "You may want to, Edwin, but once the battle starts there'll be no time for doing anything other than looking after yourself."

CHAPTER FIVE

Osric and I didn't get the chance to talk much more during our journey south to London. For one thing, once we'd made camp for the night, my father kept me practising with sword, spear and shield until it was time for sleep.

"It's important you are prepared," he told me. "Your life will be at stake on the battlefield."

The other reason was that Osric's father, Lord Bane, seemed to be keeping a very close watch on his son; almost as if he was worried that Osric might run away. I knew there was no chance of that happening, Osric was too honest to do something like that. But with Lord Bane always so close, there was no real chance for me and Osric to talk more about his situation.

As my father predicted, it took our army ten days to reach London. Once there, the King and his marshal set about gathering more troops. The marshal estimated that it would take about a week to bring our army up to strength. So my father and I, and Lord Bane and Osric, set off for our homes in Kent, along with our own soldiers, to meet up with our families and make sure that things at home were in order, before we set off south to Hastings.

Every English lord was expected to raise his own army of soldiers from among the workers on his estate, ready for service to the King. This meant that most of the soldiers in King Harold's army were actually farm labourers, drawn from the strongest and bravest. Give them a shield, a sword or an axe, and they were an army powerful enough to face any enemy. Only the lord, earls, squires and senior servants, such as my father's steward, Ulric, were trained as warriors.

We reached the crossroads outside Sevenoaks in the late afternoon, and then my father and our soldiers headed for our home, while Osric, Lord Bane and his soldiers made their way to Otford. The goodbye between myself and Osric was brief, and under Lord Bane's watchful stare, but I made sure to say loudly to Osric "I'll come and see you in a day or so!" to let Lord Bane know that I would not be frightened away by his harsh manner.

When we arrived back at the field gates that marked the entrance to Wolf Court, our family home, Ulric dismissed the soldiers, who all rushed off, eager to be back with their families once more. We had all been away from home for a long time. Some of our soldiers had returned to work the land during the harvest in September, but many – as was the case with my father and I – had been in arms with King Harold since early July, and it was now early October. It had been a long three months.

My father and I rode our horses along the track, and as we neared our house, with its walls of thick wooden beams and clay, its thatched roof and tall chimneys, I saw the door open and my two sisters, Emma and Mary, rush out to greet us.

"Get back!" called my father to them, and they turned and ran back towards the house to join our mother, who was now also hurrying out.

We pulled our horses to a halt outside the front door and jumped down. Emma, who was ten, grabbed me round the waist and hugged me, burying her head in my chest.

"Oh Edwin!" she said. "We wondered if you were dead!"

"No, I am quite alive," I said.

"We heard reports that many had died," said my mother.

She went to my father and took his hand and squeezed it, relief writ on her face.

"I am sorry, Margaret," my father apologized to her. "I should have sent a messenger on ahead with the news that we were safe."

"Yes, you should have!" scolded my mother.

"Did you have a good battle?" demanded Mary, who was six.

My father looked down at her, then picked

her up and cuddled her to him, an unhappy smile on his face.

"There are no good battles, my sweet," he said sadly. "Only battles that are lost or won."

The nurse appeared from the house, carrying my baby brother, Edgar, and I was surprised to see how big he was.

"Edgar has grown!" I said. "He was so tiny when we went away!"

"He was barely born then," said my mother. "And now, it is nearly four months since we have seen you, or had word of you."

"Three months," corrected my father.

"It feels much longer," said my mother.

CHAPTER SIX

And so we returned home. It felt good to spend time with my sisters again, to be in the familiar and comfortable surroundings of our house, and finally to get to sleep in my own bed. That night I slept easier and for longer than I had in months.

The next day, after training in the early morning, I went with my father and Ulric and we rode around the estate, checking on the families who worked for us, making sure that they were well and that they all had food stored and wood for their fires. There were many different sorts of lord: there were those who ruled their estates by fear and the threat of severe punishments, such as whipping; and there were those like my father. He cared for the people who worked his lands and did his best to make sure they were kept healthy and safe. If a cottage needed repairing, he made sure the work was done. If one of his workers, or their family, fell ill he made sure a wise woman was sent for to give them her medicines.

I once overheard a conversation between my father and Lord Bane, when Lord Bane snapped at my father: "You are too soft with your workers, Wolf. You pamper them! Word spreads. It makes it hard for those of us who believe in discipline to keep order!"

"There is discipline," my father corrected him. "But it is different from yours. My people appreciate the way I treat them. In return, they work hard for me because they know it is their side of the bargain."

As we went from cottage to cottage, I could see the affection the people had for my father. And at each place he spent time talking to them, listening to them. It was late afternoon by the time we headed back towards Wolf Court.

"Bear this in mind Edwin," said my father. "One day you will inherit this estate, and you will become Lord Wolf. Treat the people who work for you as I do, as human beings with feelings, not as slaves, and they will work much harder for you."

Next morning I spent time with my sisters, and also watching my baby brother, Edgar. In the afternoon I set out for Otford, to see Osric as I'd promised. I was worried about my friend. He was so unhappy at the thought of going into battle, but I knew that he would die rather than not take up the challenge. His family's honour was too important to him.

Bane Hall looked similar to our house — the same wood and clay construction, the same thatched roof — but the atmosphere was very different. The workers I passed in the fields as I rode towards the main house kept their eyes down, and when I reached the house there was no rush of people to greet visitors, as there was at ours, with Emma and Mary running out like wild animals.

I got down from my horse and tethered it, then rang the small iron bell that hung by the front door. After a while, the door opened and the Banes' house servant, Ivar, appeared. I had known Ivar since I was tiny, and he rarely smiled. He didn't smile now, just said "Master Edwin?"

"Good afternoon, Ivar," I said. "I have come to see Master Osric."

"He is in the courtyard with Lord Bane," said Ivar.

"Thank you," I said.

I walked the length of the house, and round the corner into the courtyard at the back, where the stables and outbuildings were.

Osric was in full armour with a heavy sword in both hands, engaged in combat with

one of Lord Bane's soldiers, also in armour.
Lord Bane stood and watched, his face grim,
as Osric advanced, bringing his sword down
on the soldier's shield with a crash. The soldier
stumbled slightly, moved back, then advanced
on Osric with his own sword.

At one side of the courtyard, sitting together on a long wooden bench and watching this, were Osric's mother, Lady Bane, his three sisters, Hetta, Elgiva and Gytha, and his brother, Aidan. As they saw me, they all rose to their feet, a movement that caused Lord Bane to turn. He saw me, frowned, and shouted "Halt!" to Osric and the soldier, who immediately stopped their combat.

"Edwin," Lord Bane greeted me gruffly.

"Good afternoon, Lord Bane," I said, with a bow. "And to Lady Bane and your family."

I bowed to them. They, in turn, replied: Lady Bane and the three girls with small curtsies, and Aidan with a deep bow.

"I have come to see Osric, if that is permissible," I said.

Lord Bane hesitated, scowled, then said: "Very well. We shall take a break from his training. But not for too long. We have important business ahead of us."

He turned to his wife and children and snapped brusquely: "Come!"

With that, he headed for the house, followed in silence by Lady Bane, Hetta, Elgiva, Gytha and Aidan.

I helped Osric remove his armour, while the soldier disappeared into the stables to go about other business.

"My father hates me," scowled Osric.

"I'm sure he doesn't," I said. "He only puts you through this to make sure you're ready when we go into battle."

"He doesn't want me to let him down, that's all," said Osric. "His good name is more important to him than anything. Or any of us. He treats us all badly."

I thought of my father and the way he was with my sisters and me, and with the people who worked for him. I knew that

Osric was right, and thought how sad it was that we couldn't choose our parents.

"How is the training going?" I asked.

"As always, well enough," shrugged Osric. "I can handle a sword and a spear and a shield, but I don't wish to. And that is what my father refuses to hear."

We sat down on the long wooden bench and talked, although in truth most of our conversation consisted of Osric complaining about his father, and how badly he wanted to live a life of learning and books, with me making sympathetic noises.

"There is more to this life than fighting and wars, Edwin," he said. "There are mysteries to be solved. Why does the sun rise in the morning? Where does it go at night? Why are days shorter in the winter than summer? Where do birds go to in winter?"

"I have no idea," I said. "These things

just happen."

"But why?" asked Osric.

We talked for another hour or so, until Lord Bane reappeared and shouted for the soldier, who came out of the stables.

"At least I don't have to perform in front of the family audience this time," muttered Osric. "Mother doesn't like it, nor do the others. But father makes them watch."

"To give you support?" I suggested.

"No," said Osric. "It's to show his power over everyone."

As Osric put on his armour, I took my leave of him, and Bane Hall, and returned home. As I left the Bane estate, I felt a sense of relief to be leaving that stifling and unhappy place and returning to the fresh air and happiness of Wolf Court.

CHAPTER SEVEN

Two days after I'd watched Osric train at Bane Hall, messengers arrived from the King summoning us all to rejoin him as he rode with his re-formed army south on the road to Hastings.

Once more, my father and I said goodbye to my mother and sisters, and baby Edgar. We gathered up our soldiers from among our workers, with Ulric as their marshal, and set off. We met Osric and Lord Bane and his men at the Sevenoaks crossroads, and continued south to join the main body of King Harold's army. We were back to strength: thousands of men, armed and ready for battle.

As we journeyed south towards Hastings, we received reports that the Normans had built two large castles outside Hastings and Pevensey on the south coast. The Duke and his royal court and senior nobles stayed in them, while most of their soldiers camped outside. The attacks by local English on the Normans had stopped because the English forces had withdrawn into the countryside and were waiting to join King Harold and our main army when we arrived. There had been no attempt by Duke William to move further north towards London, or to spread further out from Hastings. William was obviously waiting for King Harold to come to him.

Every day when we halted, Osric was put through training by his father. Sometimes I watched him going through his paces. Each time, Osric showed that he had the skill with weapons, but one look at his face and anyone could see his heart wasn't in it. And that worried me. A warrior who doesn't have the heart and desire to fight is more likely to die in battle than one who does.

It was on 13th October that we finally arrived at Caldbec Hill, a ridge about eight miles from Duke William's castle outside Hastings, where we made our camp.

Caldbec Hill was a high place. In the distance I could see smoke rising from the fires in the Norman camp, and through the smoke I could make out the shape of the castle that had been built for Duke William.

"Their army is huge," said a voice beside me.

It was Osric. He had managed to slip away from the watchful eye of his father. Lord Bane, like my father, was busy arranging our army for the battle that was to come.

"It looks no bigger than our army," I said.

"But they will be fresher than ours," said

Osric. "Our men have marched 300 miles north, fought a fierce battle, and then marched 300 miles back again. Many of them carry wounds. The Normans have had time to get themselves fit."

"But King Harold has chosen this place for our position. He is inviting the Normans to attack us. They will have to come to us uphill. We will have the advantage."

"Only if they launch an attack," said Osric. "Duke William may wait for us to attack him. And he has a castle to hide in."

"A castle made of wood," I reminded him. "It will burn, forcing him out."

"Edwin!" I turned and saw my father coming towards us.

"The King is holding a council of war," he told us. "As my squire, and now a warrior, you will join us."

"I will be honoured, father," I said.

My father turned to Osric.

"Your father is looking for you, Osric," he said. "I suggest you join us as well."

"Yes, Lord Wolf," said Osric, making a small bow as he did so.

Osric and I followed my father along the ridge to the King's tent. Other nobles were already clustering into the tent. I saw Lord Bane scanning the area around the tent, an anxious look on his face, which cleared as he saw Osric. He hailed for Osric to accompany him, and Osric gave me a sad and desperate smile and hurried to join his father.

Inside the tent, King Harold was talking earnestly to his two brothers, the Earls Leofwine and Gyrth Godwinson, but they stopped talking as my father and the other nobles began to fill out the tent. Proudly, I stood next to my father.

"Earlier today I sent an emissary to Duke

William," announced King Harold.

Often, before a battle, messengers would be sent under a flag of truce to the enemy with demands, either for surrender, or terms for a peaceful settlement. Rarely was a battle prevented from happening. In some cases, the messengers were slaughtered and their bodies sent back as an added insult.

"I demanded that he and his army return to Normandy and have no further interest in England. He refused. And so the battle will take place."

"Do we know when, your Majesty?" asked Lord Bane.

"It could be tomorrow," said King Harold. "He knows we have just arrived here today, and I doubt if he will want to give us time to firm up our defences."

"It would help if we knew their plan of battle," murmured Earl Gyrth. "Then we could make proper preparations. The Normans will be fresher than our men, and we'll need every advantage we can take if we are to beat them."

As I heard these words, an outrageous thought struck me. I could speak French. I could get into the French camp and find out their plans. But to say such a thing in front of the King and these great warriors might be taken as insolent: a mere boy poking his nose into warrior business. But the future of England was at stake. I took a deep breath.

"I could find out their plans," I said.

Beside me, I felt my father tense. He looked down at me, his face grim and angry. It was one thing for me to be in attendance as a squire, but I could tell he felt I'd overstepped my situation by speaking. But now, I told myself, I was a warrior. I had the right as a warrior and the son of a lord to speak.

The King looked at me.

"You?" he queried. "A boy?"

"It is because I am a boy that I will be able to move among the enemy easier than a grown man, your Majesty," I said. "And I speak their language. They will think I am one of their own."

"Edwin was educated by monks, your

Majesty," put in my father. "Including monks from Normandy."

Now he saw that the King was not angry at my having spoken up, but intrigued, he felt able to add his voice to mine.

"I'm sure I can pass for a Norman, your Majesty," I said; but I said it in French.

The King's face broke into a grin.

"Well, well!" he smiled. "It seems we have a secret weapon!" Then his face grew serious. "But this will be a dangerous mission. If you are caught, they will not treat you kindly."

"I know the danger, your Majesty," I said. "But the bigger danger is not defeating the invader."

King Harold turned to my father and nodded. "I like your son, Lord Wolf," he said. "He has courage and intelligence. If I had a hundred more like him, we would drive this invader back into the sea tomorrow."

CHAPTER EIGHT

While the others stayed to discuss tactics for the forthcoming battle, I was told to go and prepare myself for my secret foray into the Norman camp. I would need to remove anything from my clothes that might give away that I was English, and then dress myself as a Norman would. It had been decided that I should pretend to be just a house servant or kitchen boy, because a Norman page or squire would be wearing badges and ribbons showing which master he served. As a lowly kitchen boy I could just wear nondescript rags.

I was walking away from the King's tent,

when I heard Osric call my name. I turned and waited for him as he hurried up to me.

"Let me go with you, Edwin!" he said.

I looked at him, surprised.

"I thought you didn't want to take part in warfare," I said.

"What you are planning is not open battle," said Edwin. "I can do this. And I speak French as well as you do. Even better!"

That was true. Osric was a better scholar than I was.

"I don't know," I said doubtfully. "I'm planning to go among them saying I am looking for my brother. That may be less believable if there are two of us."

"Not necessarily," argued Osric. "And it will mean there will be two of us, with one ready to go and get help if we run into trouble."

"If we run into trouble we will not be

able to get out," I pointed out. "There are thousands of Norman soldiers, and our camp is eight miles away."

"Yes, but I'm sure I will be of use!" insisted Osric.

"Osric!" snapped a deep and angry voice.

We turned to see Lord Bane glaring at us.

"Father, I wish to go with Edwin to the Norman camp," said Osric. "I want to help discover the Normans' battle plans."

"No," said Lord Bane, and to my surprise there was clear anger in his voice.

"But, Father…" Osric began to appeal, but he was cut short.

"Even though the King has given his permission for what Edwin intends to do, I do not approve," snapped Lord Bane. He turned and glared at me. "Sneaking and spying is not honourable! There is only one honourable way in battle, and that is one warrior face to face with another."

With that he turned and walked off, with a curt command: "Come, Osric!"

Osric looked at me with an apologetic expression on his face, and then followed his father away, his shoulders hunched miserably.

I felt a hand on my shoulder and turned to see that my father had arrived.

"You will need to be more alert than that if you are to survive," said my father. "Your attention was lost and I was able to sneak up on you. If that had been a sword instead of my hand on your shoulder, you would have been dead."

I bowed my head.

"I am sorry, Father," I said. "You are right."

"But you were upset by what Lord Bane said to you," nodded my father, understanding. Then he shook his head. "Let that be a lesson to you. Don't allow yourself to be distracted by anything, or you will die."

"But what Lord Bane said…" I blurted out.

"Is his opinion," said my father in a firm tone. "Lord Bane has many opinions which are different from mine. In this case, what is important is the opinion of the King, and the King approves." He looked down at me, his face serious. "This will be a good test of your bravery and wits, Edwin. You will be alone, surrounded by a dangerous enemy, thousands of them. If things go wrong for you, there will be no chance of us finding out the worst has happened and coming to your rescue."

"I understand," I said.

Once again, he put his hand on my shoulder, but this time his touch was gentler.

"Be careful and stay alive, my son," he said.

CHAPTER NINE

After having changed into rough clothes
suited to a servant boy, I rode my horse
to within a mile of the Norman camp. I
tethered it to a tree and made the rest of the
journey on foot across countryside. Keeping
to hedges and narrow tracks, I reached a
small wood about half a mile away from
their camp just as darkness was falling. I
peered out from the cover of the trees and
bushes. Even in this half-light of dusk I could
see that the Norman camp was enormous,
stretching across open ground for at least a
mile to the high walls of the huge wooden
castle. Inside that castle, so I'd been told,

were the Norman Duke William and his knights. The ordinary soldiers were spread across the vast area. I could see their tents and horses, and large fires burning to keep them warm and cook their food. The soldiers sat in groups, or walked about.

I looked for guards at the edge of the camp, but there were very few, just an occasional pair of soldiers set at long distances and armed with spears, supposedly keeping watch but mainly – it seemed to me – talking. They appeared very relaxed about keeping guard. But then, why wouldn't they? They knew where the English camp was: on the ridge at Caldbec Hill, eight miles away. If an attack was launched, then it would be easily seen: thousands of men could not be hidden so easily. All it needed was one shout from one of the guards, and the whole camp would spring into action. But they would not be watching for one boy. At least, that is what I hoped.

I crawled along the ground until I was at a point halfway between two guard-posts, and then I continued, moving slowly, stopping every now and then to check if the guards were alert to my coming. I made it through the gap between the guard-posts, and carried on crawling until I reached a small clump of bushes. Once there, I stood up, brushed the leaves and grass off my clothes, and surveyed the scene inside the Norman camp.

The enormous size of the camp, many thousands of men, didn't daunt me; our own camps were just as large, and I had grown up as my father's page close to large armies and battles. My worry was that I would be spotted as an imposter, as an English spy. Even though I had learnt French from my tutors, I wasn't as fluent in it as someone like Osric. My best chance would to be to pretend to be not very bright, in that way any stumbles in my speech would be excused as my being a simpleton.

I headed for nearest fire and the soldiers gathered around it. As I drew near a soldier stepped in front of me, barring my path, and pointed a spear at me, and – in French – ordered me to stop. So, they had guards on duty inside the camp.

I stopped and forced a friendly smile. The guard didn't smile back.

"What are you doing?" he demanded.

"I'm looking for my brother," I said. "His name's Pierre."

The guard frowned.

"Who?" he asked.

"We got separated earlier today," I told him.

"Who are you with?"

This was the question I'd been dreading. According to the information my father had been able to pass on to me, the Norman Duke had four different regiments of soldiers with him. One was his own army, the others were led by Alan the Red, William FitzOsbern, and the last by Eustace, the Count of Boulogne. If I said the name of one of them, and that turned out to be the very group I'd walked into, I'd soon be proved a liar. But there was one other group made up of priests and servants, who weren't expected to take part in the actual fighting.

"He said if we got separated he'd be with the priests, but I don't know where they are."

I gave him a helpless and miserable look, and he lowered his spear and nodded.

"Right now they'll be busy praying for our victory," he said. He hesitated, then he obviously took pity on me because he asked:

"Have you eaten?"

I shook my head.

"Why don't you come and have a bowl of stew with us? It'll warm you up on a cold night like this. Then after I'll take you to where the priests are and you can find your brother."

"Thank you," I smiled gratefully.

I followed the soldier to the big roaring fire. A large cauldron was hanging from a spit over the fire, and a cook was serving stew into wooden bowls. My new soldier friend took a bowl of stew himself, and then handed one to me.

"Come on," he said. "Let's join my friends."

Carrying the bowl, I followed him to where a small group of soldiers were sitting together, soaking up the liquid from the stew with bread and scooping the meat into their mouths with their fingers. I sat down with them and began to eat in the same way. The stew tasted good, and I suddenly realized how hungry I was. I hadn't eaten nearly all day.

The other soldiers looked at me curiously.

"Who's this?" asked one.

"He got separated from his brother," said the guard. "He says his brother's with the priests, and right now they'll be fasting as part of their prayer for victory. I thought he wouldn't get any food there, so he might as well have a bite with us."

One of the other soldiers laughed.

"That's true!" he chuckled. He grinned at me. "Take my tip, boy. Stay with us. You'll get better fed than if you're with the priests."

The others joined in the laughter at this, and one added: "Mind, you'll find it a bit tougher with us than with the priests. While they're down on their knees praying for victory, we're in the middle of the action making sure the victory happens!"

This caused even more laughter. Then one of the soldiers asked me: "You ever been in a battle, boy?"

I shook my head.

"No," I said. "I'm a servant. My brother said this was my chance to see our army victorious."

"Your brother's right," nodded one of the men. "King Harold and his men will fall apart once we attack."

I gave a shrug. I wasn't going to reveal myself, but I couldn't let that pass.

"My brother says the English fight well," I said. "He says they defeated the Vikings."

"And that's their problem," said one of the men. "They won't have the strength for another big battle so soon after the last one. And that long march south they've just done will have killed them."

"And there's a big difference between the way Duke William's army go about battle and the way the Vikings do."

"Our archers," nodded a man. "They rain arrows down on the enemy. Death from the skies. No one can stand against those arrows coming down."

"And then, when our arrows have laid most of them low, that's when we go in." And he picked up his spear and waved it above his head, while another man pulled his sword from its scabbard and held it high, before replacing it.

"We're the infantry," said the man proudly. "Foot soldiers. Hand-to-hand combat. We break them down, open up a gap in their front line, and then the cavalry come in."

"After we've done all the hard work," put in another, his tone complaining.

"And then, if we can't break through their lines, then we do the old running away trick". And he winked and the other men chuckled and grinned broadly.

"What's the old running away trick?" I asked.

"It's the oldest trick in the book," said the man, "So old they reckon the Romans used it. Say the enemy is holding firm and we can't get an opening in their defences. That's likely with the English — they do this thing called a shield wall, where they lock the edges of their wooden shields together so it makes a kind of wall they hide behind."

I knew what he meant. I'd seen the shield wall in action at Stamford Bridge.

"Well, if that happens, then we charge at 'em, and then turn round and run away, like we've given up and are retreating. Sure enough, time after time, the enemy think we're beaten and chase after us. And once they do that, we stop and turn and face 'em, and then our cavalry charge at them and cut them down." He smiled broadly. "Works every time!"

"Nearly every time," another man corrected him. "I've known times when the enemy haven't chased after us."

"All right, nearly every time," conceded the first man.

"And when will the battle start?" I asked.

At this there was an awkward strained silence, and I wondered if I'd asked too much. It was a stupid question to ask, too obvious.

"Two days. Three?" I added quickly, hoping to show my ignorance. "I want to make sure I find my brother before the battle starts."

"Your brother hasn't told you?" asked one of the men, puzzled.

I looked back at him, doing my best to look equally puzzled.

"Told me what?" I asked.

The men exchanged looks, then shrugged.

"Maybe his brother wants to keep him right away from it," he said.

"I'm still surprised no one told him," said another.

"Told me what?" I repeated.

"The battle begins tomorrow. We attack at first light."

CHAPTER TEN

Tomorrow at first light! As these words sank in, I knew it was important that I get back to our own camp as fast as possible to warn the King. But how could I get away from these men without raising their suspicion?

Fortunately, the answer came in the helpful guard who'd first found me.

"Well, young man, now you've finished your stew, we ought to go and find your brother," he said.

"Thank you," I said, and scrambled to my feet.

The problem I now had was how to get away from him, and how to stop myself being taken to where the priests and servants were stationed. Once I was there, my lie would soon be exposed. No one would be my brother, no one would recognize me. I would be captured and questioned. And questioning, if the answers weren't forthcoming, often meant torture.

We set off towards the part of the huge camp where the priests and servants were based, me following the French soldier. As we neared that section of the camp, I suddenly stopped and blurted out: "There he is!"

"What, your brother?" asked the guard.

"Yes!" I said. Then I waved and shouted out: "Pierre!"

At my shout, some of the men in the camp turned to look at me, but I turned back to the guard.

"He must have come looking for me!" I said. "Thank you!"

And then I ran towards the area where the priests and servants were. Behind me, the guard muttered something "Good luck". I turned to wave him farewell, and saw that he was already heading back to rejoin his companions by his own campfire.

I saw that some of the people in the priests' and servants' area were still watching me, so I set off after the departing guard, and immediately they seemed to lose interest in me. I stopped, looked around, and spotted a clump of trees and bushes towards the outer area of the camp. I walked over to this clump, as if I was heading that way to use it as a toilet, but once I was there I dropped down to the ground.

By now it was completely dark outside the areas of the fires, whose flames lit up the camp. Now I had to get out of the camp, past the guards. Once again, as I had done before,

I began to crawl over the ground, moving slowly. As I did, my eyes adjusted to the dark. What had been just blackness became shapes and shades of darkness. I remembered my father's words about staying alert, and kept my eyes and ears sharp for sounds and moving shapes. I crawled, feeling brambles tugging at my clothes, sharp thorns digging and tearing at my skin.

I had to get back to the English camp! I had to warn the King and my father that the Norman attack was just hours away!

I moved slowly, guessing and hoping that I must be nearing the edge of the Norman camp. And then I stopped as I heard voices. Two men, Normans, obviously on guard duty, and my heart pounded as I heard one say: "I heard something moving."

In the darkness, I could just make out the shapes of two men, and one of them was pointing a spear in my direction.

"I can't hear anything," said the other.

"It's stopped now," said the first. "But it sounded big."

"It must be an animal."

"An animal means meat," said the other. "I've been living on oats and turnips for too long."

In the gloom, I saw the man raise his spear.

"What are you doing?" demanded the other guard.

"What's it look like I'm doing! I'm going to kill me something to eat!"

And then I saw his arm move. Frantically, I rolled forward and sideways, and just in time, because the spear thudded into the ground where I'd been hiding just a second before. I carried on rolling, and then began to run, crouching low. I heard one of the men groan and say "It's gone!", then the other ask: "What sort of animal d'you reckon it was?"

I carried on running as fast as I could, stumbling now and then on the uneven ground, and sometimes falling, but always driving myself on.

Finally, when I felt I'd gone far enough, I stopped and looked back, listening. The guards and the Norman camp were behind me. Now to get to my horse and back to the King with my information.

CHAPTER ELEVEN

My father and Lord Bane, and the other lords, stood with the King in his tent and listened as I told them what I had learnt in the Norman camp.

"Archers, infantry and then cavalry," murmured King Harold thoughtfully after I'd finished.

"We have learnt nothing new, your Majesty," growled Lord Bane glaring sourly at me. "Archers and infantry followed by cavalry is the Norman way in battle."

"With respect, Lord Bane," said my father quietly, "I believe Edwin has brought us two things we did not know before tonight. The first is their ruse of pretending to run away to draw our shield wall to break up."

"An old trick," snorted Lord Bane.

"And the second," continued my father, "is the fact that the Normans will launch their attack at first light, in just a few hours."

"Indeed, Lord Wolf," nodded the King. "And, for that alone, your son is to be praised for his bravery. Do you not agree, Lord Bane?"

All eyes turned to Lord Bane, who scowled uncomfortably, before admitting in reluctant tones: "Indeed, your Majesty."

"The Normans have many archers," put in Earl Gyrth. "We should have brought more with us."

"I disagree, Earl Gyrth," said another. "Our shield wall can protect against their arrows. Archers need arrows for their bows. With few in our ranks to supply them, their arrows will soon be used up."

"What is important is that our shield wall holds, and we keep the high ground" said my father. "The Normans will suffer heavy losses battering themselves against our defences. Eventually they will tire and weaken."

"And then we will strike at them," nodded the King. "Good. Go and prepare our forces. Place them in their positions. Make sure every man is ready, and knows his duty when daylight comes. The Battle at Stamford Bridge was hard, but this, I feel, will be much harder."

As my father and I left the King's tent, he patted me on the shoulder.

"You did well, my son," he said, "I am proud of you."

"Lord Bane does not agree with you," I said.

My father fell silent, then said carefully: "Lord Bane is a person to be careful of,

Edwin. He had to admit he was wrong front of others just now. He will bear you a grudge for that. When this battle is over and we have won, if anything should happen to me, be careful of Lord Bane."

"Nothing will happen to you, father," I insisted. "When the battle comes, this time I will be by your side. I will protect you!"

At this, my father laughed.

"Oh Edwin," he said. "If only it were that simple!"

CHAPTER TWELVE

The next morning we rose well before dawn, to make sure that everybody ate a good breakfast. I'd had very little sleep because of my late return from the Norman camp, and we had a long and hard day ahead of us, and did not know when we would eat again.

The first thing those of us who wore armour did on rising was to put on our chain-mail shirts, called hauberks, and arm ourselves with our weapons. We did not want to be caught unarmed if the Normans should launch a surprise attack, and although we had our look-outs high on the ridge, their eyes on the Norman camp in the distance, it was still dark, and the area around us was heavily wooded. An army could creep through the woods in the darkness and be upon us before we would have been aware of it.

The chain-mail shirt was heavy, made up of small metal rings linked together. If an enemy struck you with his sword, the chain mail was supposed to stop the blade of the sword from cutting in to you. The thing it wouldn't stop was the heavy iron blade breaking a bone if the blow was hard enough. To protect our heads we wore metal helmets. One problem was that if a sword blow glanced off it, it was likely to smash down on your shoulder and break your collarbone. And, although the helmet was made of metal, a really hard blow could cut into it.

We also had round shields made of thick wood, which would take a blow from a sword. One problem with the shields was that if the enemy stabbed at you with a spear, the point of the spear could go in to the wood and get stuck. If that happened, the only way to deal with it was to strike at the enemy with your sword while he was stuck.

My own particular weapon was a sword. It was smaller than the sword my father and the other warrior-lords used because I was still young, but I had perfected the thrusting action in practice, using it more like a long dagger. I could make my thrust while my opponent was still lifting his sword up, ready to crash it down on me. Because my opponent would also be wearing a chain-mail shirt covering his body and arms, it meant aiming my sword thrust at points where his body was exposed: his face and throat.

A lot of King Harold's inner army, the housecarls who formed a protective ring around him during battle, favoured the two-handed battleaxe. This was a fierce and heavy weapon with two sharp blades, but as it needed two strong arms to hold and swing it, they were not able to use shields for their own protection. Most of them kept their shield slung on a strap hanging down behind their back, and a sword by their side, so that if the fighting got too close to be able to swing the battleaxe effectively, they changed to sword and shield.

As I sat eating my breakfast of bread and meat, my head was filled with thoughts of the battle to come – my first battle. I had spent many years training, learning to use a sword, a spear and an axe, but for the most part they had been blunted. Now I would be going into battle against older and hardened warriors, facing sharp swords and spears, and people who wanted to kill me, not just disarm me in a training bout. How would I fare? Would I survive? If I did, would I be damaged? Would I lose an arm or a leg or my eyes, like so many former soldiers I had seen begging on streets in towns and villages?

As I ate, I became aware of someone sitting down beside me. It was Osric. I looked past him for his father, Lord Bane, but he was not there. I guessed he was with the King, as was my father, talking final tactics before the battle.

"Are you ready for the battle?" I asked.

Osric shook his head.

"No," he said. "I don't want to fight, but I have to, otherwise I will shame my father's name as a coward." He looked miserable. "I will die today."

"You are too clever to die," I said. "You are quick. You think quickly. All you have to do is watch out for people attacking you, and dodge them."

"There will be nowhere to dodge them," said Osric with a sigh. "You know what it is like in battle, Edwin: the men packed tightly together. There is nowhere for anyone to turn, let alone move and dodge."

"The line always breaks when the battle is at its height," I said.

"I want to run away," said Osric.

I hesitated. I did not know what to say. If he ran away then he would be an outcast from his father and his family. But if he stayed, then it was possible that he would die; just as was the case with all of us.

"Run away," I told him suddenly. "You are right, the life of a soldier is not for you. You should be a monk. A teacher."

Osric sighed.

"No," he said. "I could not bring that shame on my father."

I held out my platter, with bread and meat on it, towards him.

"Have you had breakfast?" I asked.

Osric shook his head.

"No," he said. "I feel too sick to eat."

"Edwin," said my father's voice.

I looked up at him. In his chain mail, and with his shield slung across his back and his long sword in its scabbard hanging by his side, he looked every part the fine warrior, and I felt proud to be going into battle alongside him.

"We are ready," he said. "It is time to take our places."

CHAPTER THIRTEEN

As I stood up, Lord Bane appeared and gave Osric a glare. In one hand he gripped the shaft of his favoured two-handed axe.

"Come!" he snapped.

Then he turned and walked off, axe held firmly, his sword dangling at his side. Osric got to his feet and went after his father, his head down, a miserable expression on his face.

I followed my father to the high point of the ridge. Our front-line soldiers were already there, hundreds and hundreds of men in two enormous long lines along the ridge, facing outwards, the two lines joined at the edges of the ridge so they became one continuous line in a stretched circle shape, able to see the enemy coming from any direction. Their large wooden shields, decorated and painted, hung from their shoulders, ready to be brought up into line for the famous shield wall.

The massive space at the top of the ridge was already filling up as we reached the outer-front line, and as we passed between the hardened, battle-scarred warriors of the front to join the rest of the army on the ridge, I felt an enormous sense of pride. I was no longer an onlooker, I was one of them − a warrior!

I followed my father and we took our places high up on the ridge, close to where the King would stand, along with his brothers, Earls Gyrth and Leofwine. Lord Bane and the other nobles had also arrived and were taking their places.

The style of the battle would be that our front-line soldiers, armed with spears and swords, would form the shield wall, in which their shields were pressed together at the sides so that they made a long and strong wooden defence. When the enemy attacked they would come up against this wall, and face spears being poked out at them through it. If any man in the front line was struck down, then the soldier behind him would take his place.

The plan was for the enemy to wear themselves out battering against the shield wall. The enemy would be at a disadvantage as they would be fighting uphill. When it was seen that the enemy showed signs of weakening, the wall would open slightly and our soldiers would pour out in small units and attack the enemy nearest, fiercely; before withdrawing back inside the wall's shelter.

Once the enemy began to lose men, then we would go on the offensive: the shield wall would move forward and attack the enemy front lines, backed up by the soldiers behind them. The King, though, had taken my information about the Normans pretending to flee and then launching a counter-attack, and had given instructions to his commanders not to go in pursuit if the Normans suddenly fled, unless they were sure the Norman retreat was real, and not a ruse.

Our army was broken down into sections, based on where the men came from, which Lord's estate and who was their master. The men of my father's estate had a Wolf's head on their shields, and followed the shouted commands of my father's steward, Ulric, who was further down the ridge from where my father and I stood. Other men from our estate, and my father's section of our army, were in the main body of the soldiers, and they would echo the shouted commands that Ulric gave. Although I had seen, from earlier battles I'd observed, that once the battle was in full cry there was little chance of hearing any shouted command, so great was the sound of metal on metal, the yells and screams of the soldiers. For that reason, for major actions, trumpets would be blown to order the soldiers forward, or to retreat. The trumpeters were spread throughout the ranks of soldiers at high points along the ridge.

The enclosure inside the shield wall was now thicker, men close to one another, but making room around them so they could unsheath their swords for action.

"I can't see!" I whispered to my father, angry at being too small to be able to see the enemy approaching. All I could see were tall men towering over me.

"I can see well enough for both of us" replied my father. "I will let you know what happens."

There was a movement of the men standing beside me, and through the crowd

I saw that the King himself had arrived with his closest earls. Their group moved past us and took up their positions at the highest point of the ridge, just above us.

We were in place. The sun was now slowly gaining height, rising in the sky. The Norman soldiers had said the attack would come at first light. It was first light now. Where were the Normans?

And then I heard in the far distance the sound of trumpets, followed by an echo from our own trumpets on the ridge.

"I see them," said my father. "The Normans are coming."

CHAPTER FOURTEEN

It was then that my father called over two of his own men who were nearest to us.

"Raise my son up so that he may see the Normans," he commanded. "I want this to be a day he will always remember, the day we defeated the invader. I want the image of the Norman army to stay with him. He must see them."

The two men grabbed me, one at each side, and then lifted me up so that I could see over the heads of the men in front of me.

I had seen large armies before, as at Stamford Bridge, but the sight I saw that morning of the 14th October 1066 was like nothing else I had ever experienced. Thousands and thousands of Norman soldiers, row after row of them, with spears held aloft. The early morning sunlight was glinting on their chain mail and their metal helmets, and the points of their spears coming towards us. And, right at the front of the foot soldiers, rows and rows of archers. Behind the foot soldiers came their cavalry: hundreds and hundreds of horses ridden by chain-mailed soldiers and knights armed with spears.

"Put him down," ordered my father, and the two men lowered me to the ground.

"Thank you," I said to the two men, and to my father.

"How do you feel?" asked my father.

"Like a warrior," I replied.

Suddenly the trumpets near to us blared out.

"Their archers are getting ready to fire," said my father.

Immediately, like the rest around us, we raised our shields so they lay flat above our heads. Then I heard the sound, like a thousand birds flying through the air, getting louder and louder, followed by the crash as their arrows fell down on our shields, their points sticking in to the wood and quivering.

We kept our shields flat above us as more arrows fell on us, then more. Some arrows managed to get through the roof of shields and struck home, downing soldiers near us, but mostly our shields kept us safe.

We heard our trumpets sound again, and lowered our shields. The first onslaught by their archers was over. Then I heard the trumpets sound again.

"Here they come!" muttered my father. "Be ready!"

I felt the men around me move slightly forward, towards the outer defensive line of our shield wall. Although I was in the middle of a mass of soldiers, and protected, I could feel the nervousness in me rising. The Norman infantry would soon be falling upon us. If our shields gave way the Normans would break through. Would I be up to the challenge of hand-to-hand combat against warriors older and bigger and stronger than myself, like the men I had been eating and talking with at the Norman camp the night before?

I heard yells and shouts from our front line, and heard the clash of metal against metal and metal against wood as the Normans crashed against our shields. The men behind me surged forward, pressing me forward, as our whole army threw itself against the enemy in support of our soldiers at the very front. We pushed and pressed, holding against the Norman onslaught, the air filled with cries and yells and the ear-splitting noise of heavy weapons crashing against each other. It was impossible for me to see what was going on, all I could do was join in with the others in pressing forward against the back of the men in front of me, with my wooden shield keeping me from being crushed. I could feel that we were actually moving forward bit by bit, one half step at a time. Was it because our front line was giving way?

"What is happening, father?" I asked, but he shook his head, he couldn't hear me above the noise of battle. Instead, he looked straight ahead, his face grim, his sword held ready.

The men in front of me were forced back, forcing me back in turn. Then they moved forward again, a whole mass of men moving as one, like the tide moving in and out from the shore.

CHAPTER FIFTEEN

I lost all track of time. I was aware that the sun had climbed higher in the sky, so a long time had passed since those first trumpets sounded to announce the start of the battle, and still I was lost in the middle of the crowd, seeing only the backs of the soldiers in front of me. And then, as we moved forward again, I became aware that the ground beneath my feet was uneven and slippery. I looked down and realized that I was stepping on the dead bodies of our fallen soldiers. And, suddenly I found myself close to the front line, with just a few rows of men between me and our shield wall. The Normans were face to face with our men, jabbing with their spears at our front line. Now and then the points of their spears would slip under the shield wall, driving into the legs of our men, and our soldiers would fall, leaving a gap in the wall, which the Normans immediately attacked fiercely.

Our front line defended strongly, attacking the Normans with their own spears, axes and swords, and all the time we pushed forward.

Suddenly I heard the distant sound of trumpets, and I saw the Norman front line begin to move back. Then their soldiers retreated further, and suddenly they turned and began to run.

"We have them!" shouted one soldier in the shield wall. "After them!"

And our soldiers began to run after the retreating Normans in pursuit. I looked at my father in alarm. Was this retreat real, or was it the trick the Norman soldiers had spoken of to try and get our shield wall to break open?

"Hold the wall!" shouted my father.

His cry was taken up by those around him, and the words were echoed along our line. The soldiers who had gone in pursuit of the Normans were too far away to hear the command to return, but the next wave of our soldiers closed up our shield wall.

Away from our front line, the Normans suddenly stopped and turned to face our chasing soldiers, and as they did so, I saw the Norman cavalry come galloping in from the side, their horses riding down our soldiers and the swords of the cavalry cutting into them.

Immediately, the Normans who'd appeared to retreat returned to the battle, throwing themselves against our soldiers who'd chased them, cutting them down, and then once more launching themselves into an attack against our front line. But our front line, our shield wall, held firm.

The battle raged for hours. I became exhausted, but daren't let myself show it for fear of letting the Normans take advantage of my tiredness. I was not alone in my exhaustion. The men around me were getting slower in their actions and reactions, as were the Normans. There were fewer sudden movements now, it was a matter of men swinging their swords or axes against one another.

And then suddenly, I was in the front line, next to my father, our shields held in front of us, locked together as part of the wall. I rocked back as the Norman swords crashed against my wooden shield, while with my sword hand I thrust at the invaders. The blade of my sword couldn't cut through the enemy chain mail, so I changed tactic, raising my sword above my head to bring it down on the enemy soldiers, but the enemy used their shields well to defend against my blows.

We pushed with our shields against the Normans and struck at them with our weapons, and they did the same, a heaving mass of armed men struggling and hacking at one another.

Suddenly I saw my father stumble, then pitch forward and fall. Immediately, a Norman thrust his spear down with great force on my father, and I saw the point of the spear sink in to his body.

A wave of anger burst inside me as I saw my father lying there. I let out a cry of rage and swung my sword at the Norman holding the spear, which was still sticking in my father's body, but another sword swung by a Norman crashed against mine, deflecting my blade downward. Before I could bring it back up, I saw another sword appear above me, saw it swinging down towards me and the next second I felt an explosion of pain in my head and I was falling... falling... falling...

CHAPTER SIXTEEN

There were no sounds.

I opened my eyes.

I was lying on my back. Above me, birds circled in the sky. Large birds, crows.

Was I dead? Was this what happened after you died?

I began to sit up, and immediately my head exploded with pain. I lay down again and closed my eyes and the pain began to subside a bit, but it still throbbed and ached.

"You are alive," said a voice.

I opened my eyes and saw Osric beside me. He still held his sword in his hand, and his face and chain mail were covered in blood.

"You have been lying there for hours," said
Osric. "I checked, and you breathed, but I
didn't know how badly you were wounded."

"My head hurts," I said.

"I'm not surprised," said Osric. He held
up a helmet, and I saw that it was mine.
There was a deep dent in the metal.

"You were lucky," said Osric. "If the

sword had gone through the metal, your skull would have been split in two."

I pushed myself up, but slowly this time. I sat there, letting the pain in my head throb. I looked around. It was gathering dusk, the daylight fading and the gloom of evening starting to descend. A whole day had passed since the battle began. Even in this fading light, as far as the eye could see there were bodies, men lying dead. And, at the thought, tears sprang to my eyes.

"My father is dead," I said.

"As is mine," said Osric.

I looked at Osric.

"You didn't run away," I said.

He shook his head.

"No," he said. "I stayed by my father's side until the end."

I looked around at the hundreds, no, thousands of dead men around us. There seemed to be very few living. Certainly no warriors, apart from us two and a few others. I could see people moving around, examining the bodies, turning them over to look at the faces.

"They are priests and servants looking for their dead masters and their soldiers," explained Osric.

"Where are the Normans?"

"They have returned to their camp. They have take may of our soldiers with them as prisoners. They are making sure there will be no counter-attack against them." His head dropped as he said: "I was lucky. They missed me because I was beneath some of our dead."

"We lost?"

Osric nodded.

"Once the King was killed, it was all over."

King Harold was dead. Osric's words filled me with a sense of shock and terrible loss.

King Harold had always seemed invincible, the warrior at the centre of every battle, the great and wise statesman ruling with a firm but fair hand over his people.

"How did he die?"

"I hear it was an arrow through his eye."

"His brothers? Earls Gyrth and Leofwine?"

"Dead, too. Most of our lords died."

"They died bravely, defending our King and our land," I said defiantly.

"It does not matter how they died," said Osric bitterly. "They are dead. The Normans have won and Duke William the Norman will rule England. "

We fell silent as the fact sank in. All our battles had been in vain. England would be under Norman rule.

"It was the Norman archers that won the battle," I said. "You said yourself, it was an arrow killed King Harold."

"No," said Osric. "It was Stamford Bridge that lost it for us. The long march there, losing all those men, and the long march back. Without that, we would have won."

I pushed myself to my feet. My head ached from where the heavy sword had smashed down on my helmet.

"Are you all right?" asked Osric, seeing me stagger slightly.

"I am alive," I said. "I will be all right later."

He and I stood there, surveying the scene in the gathering dusk. The scale of the destruction, the vast number of dead that surrounded us, was almost too much to cope with.

"What will you do now?" asked Osric.

"I shall find my father's body. I shall find his horse and I will take my father's body home and give my mother the tragic news. Then we will bury him." I looked around at the dead. "I will not let him be eaten by crows."

"The crows can have my father," said Osric.

The tone of bitterness and anger in his voice surprised me.

"But he was your father," I protested.

"I don't care," said Osric. "He was a brute to my sisters. He was a brute to me. He did not honour us in life. I will not give him false honour now he is dead. But I will help you look for your father and help you take him home. Your father was kind and wise and deserves my respect."

"Thank you, Osric," I said. "My father was indeed all the things you say he was."

"Then let us find him before it gets too dark to see, and the night predators come out," said Osric.

CHAPTER SEVENTEEN

My father's body was near to us, lying where he had fallen after I'd seen him struck down. As I looked down on him, I felt my eyes fill with tears and I fought to hold them, back.

"You can cry," said Osric, seeing the pain in my face.

"A warrior does not cry," I said.

"A warrior can cry when he looks on someone he loves who is dead," said Osric. "You stay here with him. I will go and find horses for us."

And with that he walked away, leaving me looking down at my dead father. Then, overwhelmed by grief, I sank to my knees beside my father's body, put my head on the chain-mail shirt on his chest and sobbed.

When I had cried enough and was dry of tears, I got to my feet, and became aware that Osric was standing not far away. He was holding the reins of three horses.

"They are not ours, but their owners will have no need of them," he said. "One for you, one for me, and one for your father."

"We should take your father home as well," I said. "I know the ill will there was between you, but your mother…"

I didn't finish the sentence. Osric was quiet, thinking, and then he nodded.

"Yes," he said. He gave a long sigh. "You are right, Edwin. My mother needs to see him properly buried. I will find another horse for my father."

"Do you know where his body is?" I asked.

"Yes," he said.

And so we loaded our fathers' bodies on to the horses and tied them on so they would not fall off, and began our long journey home. I was going back to Wolf Court; to my mother, Emma, Mary and baby Edgar.

The Battle of Hastings was over.

England was lost.

EPILOGUE

After the Battle of Hastings, the English continued to put up strong resistance against William's advance towards London, forcing the Norman Duke to by-pass London and continue westward along the southern bank of the River Thames to Wallingford. From there he moved north to Berkhamsted in Hertfordshire. It was at Berkhamsted that the English leaders finally surrendered.

William was crowned King of England at Westminster Abbey in London on 25th December 1066.

Despite William being made King, there were continual outbursts of uprising by the

English against the Normans over the next few years.

By 1086, the time of the completion of the Domesday Book, which listed every town and village in England, William had built strong castles over most of the country, and his powerful army kept the English subdued.

The Norman Conquest of England was complete.

Britain had been invaded before: by the Romans, Vikings, Saxons, Jutes, and Angles from northern Europe. It had been the Angles that gave their name to the country: Angleland (England). But the Norman invasion of 1066 was the last time that Britain was invaded by an army and conquered.